# SADIE'S BEACH VACATION

*Linda Zimmerman*

Copyright © 2022 Linda Zimmerman
All rights reserved.
Published by Little Blessing Books an imprint or Orison Publishers, Inc.
No part of this book may be reproduced or copied in any form
without the written permission of the publisher.
www.OrisonPublishers.com

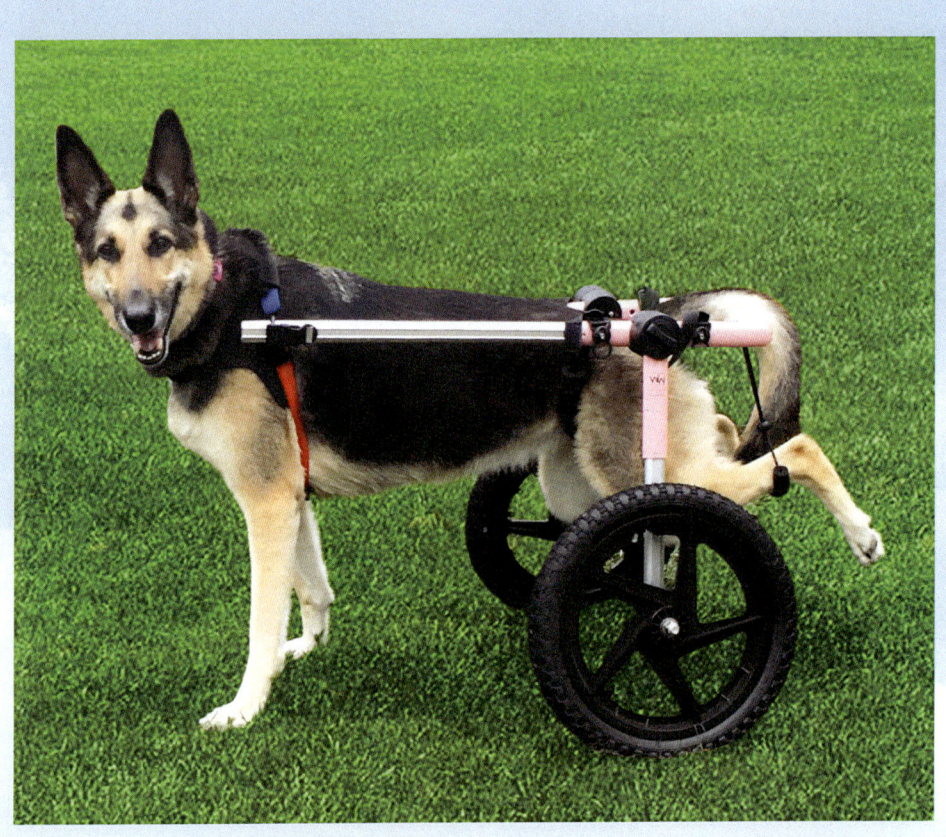

**To Sadie, you are my inspiration,
and will always have a special place in my heart.**

I am *so* excited! We are going to the beach with my cousin, Missy, and I invited Gracie along.

It's a five-hour drive, and Missy is snoring. Oh my!

I ask to trade seats with Annie, but Mom tells me to put on my earphones. Oh no! Where did I put my earphones?

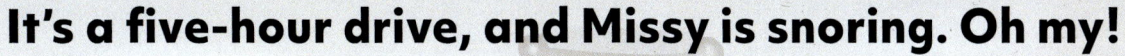

We are renting a house near the beach. It has a ramp for my wheels and lots of doggy toys!

Tonight, we eat at a seafood restaurant. Mom is so excited. But I don't see what's so special about seafood; I see food all the time!

Mom orders crabs. Not me! I don't eat anything that might pinch! Just two hot dogs and a side of ice cream for me, please.

On the Boardwalk, Annie goes to the arcade to try to win a beach ball. Missy looks for a doggy board. Gracie and I share a banana split. Oh my, Gracie has whipped cream all over her face. Ha-ha! Not me!

It's beach day! Gracie is building sandcastles, and Missy and Annie are playing with the beach ball that Annie won. I am strolling the beach in my pink wheels when I spy something orange.

Cheese Curls? They're *everywhere*!

Suddenly, I hear a loud squawk. "Scram! Those are *my* Cheese Curls!"

I look up and see a very angry sea gull with a fishhook in its beak. "Hi," I say. "I am Sadie. Who are you?"

"I'm Scrappy," the sea gull says. "What's the deal with the pink wheels?"

"My back legs are weak, and I have trouble walking, so I use wheels," I answer.

"Cool!" says Scrappy. "But you still can't have my Cheese Curls. And you need to leave now, so I can eat my lunch."

Scrappy shrugs and bites down on a Cheese Curl. "Ouch! That hurts!"

"You need soft food," I say. "I will bring you some."

"You would do that?" Scrappy replies. "You don't even know me."

"True, but you are hurting," I say. "When I was hurting, my parents, my friends, and my doctors helped me."

"Thanks, but I don't want to bother you," Scrappy says.

"You are not a bother." I say. "Do you have any favorites?"

"I could really go for some mac and cheese. Oh, and an orange smoothie." Scrappy winks.

"Vitamin C is important for supercool sea gulls like me."

"Wow, that was *super* delicious," Scrappy says, slurping the last of the smoothie.

Scrappy looks happy. But..."I can tell your beak hurts," I say. "Will you let my dad remove that fishhook?"

"I am too afraid," Scrappy whispers.

"Will you think about it?" I whisper back.

"Yes," Scrappy says, "I promise."

Scrappy is so happy he spreads his big wings and soars into the sky. Then he dives into the ocean, comes up with a crab, and drops it at my feet.

I take one look at those pinching claws and yell, "Thanks but no thanks!"

Scrappy laughs. "You don't know what you're missing! Crabs are scrumptious!"

When it is time to say good-bye, I promise to come back next summer. Scrappy says he will count the days, and he gives me my own bag of Cheese Curls. Delicious!

# MY WHEELS OF WISDOM

Help one another, even if others are different from you.

Always be patient and kind.

Do not litter. Put your trash in a trash can and recycle.

Remember, always lick your paws after eating Cheese Curls!